THE BURNING WORLD

The Burning World

by Algis Budrys

I

They walked past rows of abandoned offices in the last government office building in the world—two men who looked vastly different, but who had crucial similarities.

Josef Kimmensen had full lips trained to set in a tight, thin line, and live, intelligent eyes. He was tall and looked thin, though he was not. He was almost sixty years old, and his youth and childhood had been such that now his body was both old for its years and still a compact, tightly-wound mechanism of bone and muscle fiber.

Or had been, until an hour ago. Then it had failed him; and his one thought now was to keep Jem Bendix from finding out how close he was to death.

Jem Bendix was a young man, about twenty-eight, with a broad, friendly grin and a spring to his step. His voice, when he spoke, was low and controlled. He was the man Josef Kimmensen had chosen to replace him as president of the Freemen's League.

The building itself was left over from the old regime. It was perhaps unfortunate—Kimmensen had often debated the question with himself—to risk the associations that clung to this building. But a building is only a building, and the dust of years chokes the past to death. It was better to work here than to build a new set of offices. It might seem a waste to leave a still-new building, and that might tend to make people linger after their jobs had finished themselves. The pile of cracking bricks and peeled marble facings would be falling in a heap soon, and the small staff that still worked here couldn't help but be conscious of it. It was probably a very useful influence.

They walked through the domed rotunda, with its columns, echoing alcoves, and the jag-topped pedestals where the old regime's statues had been sledge-hammered away. The rotunda was gloomy, its skylight buried under rain-borne dust and drifted leaves from the trees on the mountainside. There was water puddled on the rotten marble floor under a place where the skylight's leading was gone.

Kimmensen had a few words with the mail clerk, and then he and Bendix walked out to the plaza, where his plane was parked. Around the plaza, the undergrowth was creeping closer every year, and vine runners were obscuring the hard precision of the concrete's edge. On all sides, the mountains towered up toward the pale sun, their steep flanks cloaked in snow and thick stands of bluish evergreen. There was a light breeze in the crystalline air, and a tang of fir sap.

Kimmensen breathed in deeply. He loved these mountains. He had been born in the warm lowlands, where a man's blood did not stir so easily nor surge so strongly through his veins. Even the air here was freedom's air.

As they climbed into his plane, he asked: "Did anything important come up in your work today, Jem?"

Jem shrugged uncertainly. "I don't know. Nothing that's urgent at the moment. But it might develop into something. I meant to speak to you about it after dinner. Did Salmaggi tell you one of our families was burned out up near the northwest border?"

Kimmensen shook his head and pressed his lips together. "No, he didn't. I didn't have time to see him today." Perhaps he should have. But Salmaggi was the inevitable misfit who somehow creeps into every administrative body. He was a small, fat, tense, shrilly argumentative man who fed on alarms like a sparrow. Somehow, through election after election, he had managed to be returned as Land Use Advisor. Supposedly, his duties were restricted to helping the old agricultural districts convert to synthetic diets. But that limitation had never restrained his busybody nature. Consultations with him were full of sidetracks into politics, alarmisms, and piping declamations about things like the occasional family found burned out.

Kimmensen despaired of ever making the old-fashioned politician types like Salmaggi understand the new society. Kimmensen, too, could feel sorrow at the thought of homesteads razed, of people dead in the midst of what they had worked to build. It was hard—terribly hard—to think of; too easy to imagine each might be his own home. Too easy to come upon the charred embers and feel that a horrible thing had been done, without taking time to think that perhaps this family had abused its freedom. Sentiment was the easy thing. But logic reminded a man that some people were quarrelsome, that some people insisted on living their neighbors' lives, that some people were offensive.

There were people with moral codes they clung to and lived by, people who worshiped in what they held to be the only orthodox way, people who clung to some idea—some rock on which their lives rested. Well and good. But if they tried to inflict these reforms on their neighbors, patience could only go so far, and the tolerance of fanaticism last just so long.

Kimmensen sighed as he fumbled with his seat belt buckle, closed the power contacts, and engaged the vanes. "We're haunted by the past, Jem," he said tiredly. "Salmaggi can't keep himself from thinking like a supervisor. He can't learn that quarrels between families are the families' business." He nodded to himself. "It's a hard thing to learn, sometimes. But if Salmaggi doesn't, one of these days he may not come back from his hoppings around the area."

"I wouldn't be worrying, Joe," Jem said with a nod of agreement. "But Salmaggi tells me there's a fellow who wants to get a group of men together and take an army into the northwest. This fellow—Anse Messerschmidt's his name—is saying these things are raids by the Northwesters."

"Is he getting much support?" Kimmensen asked quickly.

"I don't know. It doesn't seem likely. After all, the Northwesters're people just like us."

Kimmensen frowned, and for one bad moment he was frightened. He remembered, in his youth—it was only twenty-eight years ago—Bausch strutting before his cheering crowds, bellowing hysterically about the enemies surrounding them—the lurking armies of the people to the south, to the east, the northwest; every compass point held enemies for Bausch. Against those enemies, there must be mighty armies raised. Against those enemies, there must be Leadership—firm Leadership: Bausch.

"Armies!" he burst out. "The day Freemen organize to invade another area is the day they stop being Freemen. They become soldiers, loyal to the army and their generals. They lose their identification with their homes and families. They become a separate class—an armed, organized class of military specialists no one family can stand against. And on that day, freedom dies for everybody.

"You understand me, don't you, Jem? You understand how dangerous talk like this Messerschmidt's can be?" Kimmensen knew Bendix did. But it was doubly important to be doubly assured, just now.

Bendix nodded, his quick, easy smile growing on his face. "I feel the same way, Joe." And Kimmensen, looking at him, saw that Jem meant it. He had watched Jem grow up—had worked with him for the past ten years. They thought alike; their logic followed the same, inevitable paths. Kimmensen couldn't remember one instance of their disagreeing on anything.

The plane was high in the air. Below them, green forests filled the valleys, and the snow on the mountaintops was red with the light of sunset. On the east sides of the slopes, twilight cast its shadows. Kimmensen looked down at the plots of open ground, some still in crops, others light green with grass against the dark green of the trees. Off in the far west, the sun was half in the distant ocean, and the last slanting rays of direct light reflected from the snug roofs of houses nestled under trees.

Here is the world, Kimmensen thought. Here is the world we saw in the times before we fought out our freedom. Here is the world Dubrovic gave us, working in the cold of his cellar, looking like a maniac gnome, with his beard and his long hair, putting circuits together by candle-light, coughing blood and starving. Here is the world Anna and I saw together.

That was a long time ago. I was thirty-two, and Anna a worn thirty, with silver in her fine black hair, before we were free to build the house and marry. In the end, we weren't as lucky as we thought, to have come through the fighting years. The doctors honestly believed they'd gotten all the toxins out of her body, but in the end, she died.

Still, here it is, or almost. It isn't given to very many men to have their dreams come true in their lifetimes.

Kimmensen's house stood on the side of a mountain, with its back to the north and glass walls to catch the sun. There was a patio, and a lawn.

ALGIS BUDRYS

Kimmensen had been the first to break away from the old agricultural life in this area. There was no reason why a man couldn't like synthetic foods just as well as the natural varieties. Like so many other things, the clinging to particular combinations of the few basic flavors was a matter of education and nothing else. With Direct Power to transmute chemicals for him, a man was not tied to cows and a plow.

The plane settled down to its stand beside the house, and they got out and crossed the patio. The carefully tended dwarf pines and cedars in their planters were purple silhouettes against the sky. Kimmensen opened the way into the living room, then slid the glass panel back into place behind them.

The living room was shadowy and almost dark, despite the glass. Kimmensen crossed the softly whispering rug. "Apparently Susanne hasn't come home yet. She told me she was going to a party this afternoon." He took a deep, unhappy breath. "Sit down, Jem—I'll get you a drink while we're waiting." He touched the base of a lamp on an end table, and the room came to life under a soft glow of light. The patio went pitch-black by comparison.

"Scotch and water, Jem?"

Bendix held up a thumb and forefinger pressed together. "Just a pinch, Joe. A little goes a long way with me, you know."

Kimmensen nodded and went into the kitchen.

The cookers were glowing in the dark, pilot lights glinting. He touched the wall switch. The light panels came on, and he took glasses out of the cupboard. Splashing water from the ice-water tap, he shook his head with resigned impatience.

Susanne should have been home. Putting the dinner in the cookers and setting the timers was not enough, no matter how good the meal might be—and Susanne was an excellent meal planner. She ought to have been home, waiting to greet them. He wouldn't have minded so much, but she'd known Jem was going to be here. If she had to go to the Ennerth girl's party, she could have come home early. She was insulting Jem.

Kimmensen opened the freezer and dropped ice cubes into the glasses. She never enjoyed herself at parties. She always came home downcast and quiet.

Yet she went, grim-faced, determined.

He shook his head again, and started to leave the kitchen. He stopped to look inside the cookers, each with its Direct Power unit humming softly, each doing its automatic work perfectly. Once the prepared dishes had been tucked inside and the controls set, they could be left to supervise themselves. One operation followed perfectly upon another, with feedback monitors varying temperatures as a dish began to brown, with thermo-couples and humidity detectors always on guard, built into an exactly balanced system and everything done just right.

He touched the temperature controls, resetting them just a trifle to make sure, and went back out into the living room. He took the bottle of carefully compounded Scotch out of the sideboard, filled two shot glasses, and went over to Bendix.

"Here you are, Jem." He sat down jerkily, dropping rather than sinking into the chair.

Dying angered him. He felt no slowdown in his mind—his brain, he was sure, could still chew a fact the way it always had. He felt no drying out in his brain cells, no mental sinews turning into brittle cords.

He'd been lucky, yes. Not many men had come whole out of the fighting years. Now his luck had run out, and that was the end of it. There were plenty of good men long in the ground. Now he'd join them, not having done badly. Nothing to be ashamed of, and a number of grounds for quiet pride, if truth be told. Still, it made him angry.

"Susanne ought to be home any moment," he growled.

Jem smiled. "Take it easy, Joe. You know how these kids are. She probably has to wait "til somebody else's ready to leave so she can get a lift home."

Kimmensen grunted. "She could have found a way to get home in time. I offered to let her take the plane if she wanted to. But, no, she said she'd get a ride over."

The puzzled anger he always felt toward Susanne was making his head wag. She'd annoyed him for years about the plane, ever since she was eighteen. Then, when he offered her its occasional use after she'd reached twenty-five, she had made a point of not taking it. He couldn't make head or tail of the girl. She was quick, intelligent, educated—she was potentially everything he'd tried to teach her to be. But she was willful—stubborn. She refused to listen to his advice. The growing coldness between them left them constantly at swords' points. He wondered sometimes if there hadn't been something hidden in Anna's blood—some faint strain that had come to the surface in Susanne and warped her character.

No matter—she was still his daughter. He'd do his duty toward her.

"This is really very good, Joe," Jem remarked, sipping his drink. "Excellent."

"Thank you," Kimmensen replied absently. He was glaringly conscious of the break in what should have been a smooth evening's social flow. "Please accept my apologies for Susanne's thoughtlessness."

Jem smiled. "There's nothing to apologize for, Joe. When the time comes for her to settle down, she'll do it."

"Tell me, Jem—" Kimmensen started awkwardly. But he had to ask. "Do you like Susanne! I think you do, but tell me anyhow."

Jem nodded quietly. "Very much. She's moody and she's headstrong. But that'll change. When it does, I'll ask her."

Kimmensen nodded to himself. Once again, his judgment of Bendix was confirmed. Most young people were full of action. Everything had to be done now. They hadn't lived long enough to understand how many tomorrows there were in even the shortest life.

But Jem was different. He was always willing to wait and let things unfold themselves. He was cautious and solemn beyond his years. He'd make Susanne the best possible husband, and an excellent president for the League.

"It's just as well we've got a little time," Jem was saying. "I was wondering how much you knew about Anse Messerschmidt."

Kimmensen frowned. "Messerschmidt? Nothing. And everything. His kind're all cut out of the same pattern."

Jem frowned with him. "I've seen him once or twice. He's about my age, and we've bumped into each other at friends' houses. He's one of those swaggering fellows, always ready to start an argument."

"He'll start one too many, one day."

"I hope so."

Kimmensen grunted, and they relapsed into silence. Nevertheless, he felt a peculiar uneasiness. When he heard the other plane settling down outside his house, he gripped his glass tighter. He locked his eyes on the figure of Susanne walking quickly up to the living room wall, and the lean shadow behind her. Then the panel opened, and Susanne and her escort stepped out of the night and into the living room. Kimmensen took a sudden breath. He knew Susanne, and he knew that whatever she did was somehow always the worst possible thing. A deep, pain-ridden shadow crossed his face.

Susanne turned her face to look up at the man standing as quietly as one of Death's outriders beside her.

"Hello, Father," she said calmly. "Hello, Jem. I'd like you both to meet Anse Messerschmidt."

II

It had happened at almost exactly four o'clock that afternoon.

As he did at least once each day, Kimmensen had been checking his Direct Power sidearm. The weapon lay on the desk blotter in front of him. The calloused heel of his right palm held it pressed against the blotter while his forefinger pushed the buttplate aside. He moved the safety slide, pulling the focus grid out of the way, and depressed the squeeze triggers with his index and little fingers, holding the weapon securely in his folded-over palm. Inside the butt, the coil began taking power from the mysterious somewhere it was aligned on. Old Dubrovic, with his sheaves of notations and encoded symbology, could have told him. But Dubrovic had been killed in one spiteful last gasp of the old regime, for giving the world as much as he had.

A switch closed. Kimmensen released the triggers, slid the buttplate back, and pushed the safety slide down. The sidearm was working—as capable of leveling a mountain as of burning a thread-thin hole in a man.

He put the sidearm back in its holster. Such was the incarnation of freedom. The sidearm did not need to be machined out of metal, or handgripped in oil-finished walnut. These were luxuries. It needed only a few pieces of wire, twisted just so—it was an easy thing to learn—and a few transistors out of an old radio. And from the moment you had one, you were a free man. You were an army to defend your rights. And when everybody had one—when Direct Power accumulators lighted your house, drove your plane, let you create building materials, food, clothing out of any cheap, plentiful substance; when you needed no Ministry of Supply, no Board of Welfare Supervision, no Bureau of Employment Allocation, no Ministry of the Interior, no National Police—when all these things were as they were, then the world was free.

He smiled to himself. Not very many people thought of it in those technical terms, but it made no difference. They knew how it felt. He remembered talking to an old man, a year after the League was founded.

"Mr. Kimmensen, don't talk no Silas McKinley to me. I ain't never read a book in my life. I remember young fellers comin' around to court my daughter. Every once in a while, they'd get to talkin' politics with me—I gotta admit, my daughter wasn't so much. They'd try and explain about Fascism and Bureaucracy and stuff like that, and they used to get pretty worked up, throwin' those big words around. All I knew was, the government fellers used to come around and take half of my stuff for taxes. One of 'em finally come around and took my daughter. And I couldn't do nothin about it. I used to have to work sixteen hours a day just to eat.

"O.K., so now you come around and try and use your kind of big words on me. All I know is, I got me a house, I got me some land, and I got me a wife and some new daughters. And I got me a gun, and ain't nobody gonna take any of 'em away from me." The old man grinned and patted the weapon at his waist. "So, if it's all the same to you, I'll just say anything you say is O.K. by me long's it adds up to me bein' my own boss."

That had been a generation ago. But Kimmensen still remembered it as the best possible proof of the freedom he believed in. He had paid great prices for it in the past. Now that the old regime was as dead as most of the men who remembered it, he would still have been instantly ready to pay them again.

But no one demanded those sacrifices. Twenty-eight years had passed, as uneventful and unbrokenly routine as the first thirty years of his life had been desperate and dangerous. Even the last few traces of administration he represented would soon have withered away, and then his world would be complete. He reached for the next paper in his IN basket.

He felt the thready flutter in his chest and stiffened with surprise. He gripped the edge of his desk, shocked at the way this thing was suddenly upon him.

A bubble effervesced wildly in the cavity under his ribs, like a liquid turned hot in a flash.

He stared blindly. Here it was, in his fifty-ninth year. The knock on the door. He'd never guessed how it would finally come. It hadn't had to take the form of this terrible bubble. It might as easily have been a sudden sharp burst behind his eyes or a slower, subtler gnawing at his vitals. But he'd known it was coming, as every man knows and tries to forget it is coming.

The searing turbulence mounted into his throat. He opened his mouth, strangling. Sudden cords knotted around his chest and, even strangling, he groaned. Angina pectoris—pain in the chest—the second-worst pain a man can feel.

The bubble burst and his jaws snapped shut, his teeth mashing together in his lower lip. He swayed in his chair and thought:

That's it. Now I'm an old man.

After a time, he carefully mopped his lips and chin with a handkerchief and pushed the bloodied piece of cloth into the bottom of his wastebasket, under the crumpled disposal of his day's work. He kept his lips compressed until he was sure the cuts had clotted, and decided that, with care, he could speak and perhaps even eat without their being noticed. Suddenly, there were many things for him to decide quickly. He glanced at the clock on his desk. In an hour, Jem Bendix would be dropping by from his office down the hall. It'd be time to go home, and tonight Jem was invited to come to dinner.

Kimmensen shook his head. He wished he'd invited Jem for some other day. Then he shrugged, thinking: I'm acting as though the world's changed. It hasn't; I have. Some arrangements will have to change, but they will change for the quicker.

He nodded to himself. He'd wanted Susanne and Jem to meet more often. Just as well he'd made the invitation for tonight. Now, more than ever, that might be the solution to one problem. Susanne was twenty-five now; she couldn't help but be losing some of her callow ideas. Give her a husband's firm hand and steadying influence, a baby or two to occupy her time, and she'd be all right. She'd never be what he'd hoped for in a daughter, but it was too late for any more efforts toward changing that. At least she'd be all right.

He looked at his clock again. Fifty-five minutes. Time slipped away each moment your back was turned.

He hooked his mouth, forgetting the cuts, and winced. He held his palm pressed against his lips and smiled wryly in his mind. Five minutes here, five there, and suddenly twenty-eight years were gone. Twenty-eight years here in this office. He'd never thought it'd take so long to work himself out of a job, and here he wasn't quite finished even yet. When he'd accepted the League presidency, he thought he only needed a few years—two or three—before the medical and educational facilities were established well enough to function automatically. Well, they had been. Any League member could go to a hospital or a school and find another League member who'd decided to become a doctor or a teacher.

That much had been easy. In some areas, people had learned to expect cooperation from other people, and had stopped expecting some all-powerful Authority to step in and give orders. But then, medicine and education had not quite gotten under the thumb of the State in this part of the world.

The remainder had been hard. He'd expected, in a sort of naive haze, that everyone could instantly make the transition from the old regime to the new freedom. If he'd had any doubts at all, he'd dismissed them with the thought that this was, after all, mountainous country, and mountaineers were always quick to assert their personal independence. Well, they were. Except for a lingering taint from what was left of the old generation, the youngsters would be taking to freedom as naturally as they drew breath. But it had taken a whole generation. The oldsters still thought of a Leader when they thought of their president. They were accustomed to having an Authority think for them, and they confused the League with a government.

Kimmensen shuffled through the papers on his desk. There they were; requests for food from areas unused to a world where no one issued Agricultural Allocations, letters from people styling themselves Mayors of towns.... The old fictions died hard. Crazy old Dubrovic had given men everywhere the weapon of freedom, but only time and patience would give them full understanding of what freedom was.

Well, after all, this area had been drowned for centuries in the blood of rebellious men. It was the ones who gave in easily who'd had the leisure to breed children. He imagined things were different in the Western Hemisphere, where history had not had its tyrannous centuries to grind away the spirited men. But even here, more and more families were becoming self-contained units, learning to synthesize food and turn farms into parks, abandoning the marketplace towns that should have died with the first MGB man found burned in an alley.

It was coming—the day when all men would be as free of their past as of their fellow men. It seemed, now, that he would never completely see it. That was too bad. He'd hoped for at least some quiet years at home. But that choice had been made twenty-eight years ago. Sometimes a man had to be a prisoner of his own conscience. He could have stayed home and let someone else do it, but freedom was too precious to consign to someone he didn't fully trust.

Now he'd have to call a League election as soon as possible. Actually, the snowball was well on its way downhill, and all that remained for the next president was the tying up of some loose ends. The business in the outlying districts—the insistence on mistaking inter-family disputes for raids from the northwest—would blow over. A society of armed Freeman families had to go through such a period. Once mutual respect was established—once the penalty for anti-sociability became quite dear—then the society would function smoothly.

And as for who would succeed him, there wasn't a better candidate than Jem Bendix. Jem had always thought the way he did, and Jem was intelligent. Furthermore, everyone liked Jem—there'd be no trouble about the election.

So that was settled. He looked at his clock again and saw that he had a half hour more. He pushed his work out of the way, reached into a drawer, and took out a few sheets of paper. He frowned with impatience at himself as his hands fumbled. For a moment, he brooded down at the seamed stumps where the old regime's police wires had cut through his thumbs. Then, holding his pen clamped firmly between his middle and index knuckles, he began writing:

"I, Joseph Ferassi Kimmensen, being of sound mind and mature years, do make the following Will.

III

Messerschmidt was tall and bony as a wolfhound. His long face was pale, and his ears were large and prominent. Of his features, the ears were the first to attract a casual glance. Then attention shifted to his mouth, hooked in a permanent sardonic grimace under his blade of a nose. Then his eyes caught, and held. They were dark and set close together, under shaggy black eyebrows. There was something in them that made Kimmensen's hackles rise.

He tried to analyze it as Messerschmidt bowed slightly from the hips, his hands down at the sides of his dark clothes.

"Mr. President, I'm honored."

"Messerschmidt." Kimmensen acknowledge, out of courtesy. The man turned slightly and bowed to Bendix. "Mr. Secretary."

And now Kimmensen caught it. Toward him, Messerschmidt had been a bit restrained. But his bow to Jem was a shade too deep, and his voice as he delivered Jem's title was too smooth.

It was mockery. Deep, ineradicable, and unveiled, it lurked in the backs of

THE BURNING WORLD

Messerschmidt's eyes. Mockery—and the most colossal ego Kimmensen had ever encountered.

Good God! Kimmensen thought, I believed we'd killed all your kind!

"Father, I invited—" Susanne had begun, her face animated for once. Now she looked from Jem to Kimmensen and her face fell and set into a mask. "Never mind," she said flatly. She looked at Kimmensen again, and turned to Messerschmidt. "I'm sorry, Anse. You'll excuse me. I have to see to the dinner."

"Of course, Susanne," Messerschmidt said. "I hope to see you again."

Susanne nodded—a quick, sharp jerk of her head—and went quickly into the kitchen. Messerschmidt, Jem, and Kimmensen faced each other.

"An awkward situation," Messerschmidt said quietly.

"You made it," Kimmensen answered.

Messerschmidt shrugged. "I'll take the blame. I think we'd best say good night."

"Good night."

"Good night, Mr. President...Mr. Secretary."

Messerschmidt bowed to each of them and stepped out of the living room, carefully closing the panel behind him. He walked through the pool of light from the living room and disappeared into the darkness on the other side of the patio. In a minute, Kimmensen heard his plane beat its way into the air, and then he sat down again, clutching his glass. He saw that Bendix was white-lipped and shaking.

"So now I've met him," Kimmensen said, conscious of the strain of his voice.

"That man can't be allowed to stay alive!" Bendix burst out. "If all the things I hate were ever personified, they're in him."

"Yes," Kimmensen said, nodding slowly. "You're right—he's dangerous." But Kimmensen was less ready to let his emotions carry him away. The days of political killings were over—finished forever. "But I think we can trust the society to pull his teeth."

Kimmensen hunched forward in thought. "We'll talk about it tomorrow, at work. Our personal feelings are unimportant, compared to the steps we have to take as League officers."

That closed the matter for tonight, as he'd hoped it would. He still hoped that somehow tonight's purpose could be salvaged.

In that, he was disappointed. It was an awkward, forced meal, with the three of them silent and pretending nothing had happened, denying the existence of another human being. They were three people attempting to live in a sharply restricted private universe, their conversation limited to comments on the food. At the end of the evening, all their nerves were screaming. Susanne's face was pinched and drawn together, her temples white. When Kimmensen blotted his lips, he found fresh blood on the napkin.

Jem stood up awkwardly. "Well...thank you very much for inviting me, Joe." He looked toward Susanne and hesitated. "It was a delicious meal, Sue. Thank you."

"You're welcome."

"Well...I'd better be getting home..."

Kimmensen nodded, terribly disappointed. He'd planned to let Susanne fly Jem home.

"Take the plane, Jem," he said finally. "You can pick me up in the morning."

"All right. Thank you.... Good night, Sue."

"Good night"

"Joe."

"Good night, Jem." He wanted to somehow restore Bendix's s"Good night, Jem." He wanted to somehow restore Bendix's spirits. "We'll have a long talk about that other business in the morning," he reminded him.

"Yes, sir." It did seem to raise his chin a little. After Jem had left, Kimmensen turned slowly toward Susanne. She sat quietly, her eyes on her empty coffee cup.

Waiting, Kimmensen thought.

She knew, of course, that she'd hurt him badly again. She expected his anger. Well, how could he help but be angry? Hadn't any of the things he'd told her ever made any impression on her?

"Susanne."

She raised her head and he saw the stubborn, angry set to her mouth. "Father, please don't lecture me again." Every word was low, tight, and controlled.

Kimmensen clenched his hands. He'd never been able to understand this kind of defiance. Where did she get that terribly misplaced hardness in her fiber? What made her so unwilling to listen when someone older and wiser tried to teach her?

If I didn't love her, he thought, this wouldn't matter to me. But in spite of everything, I do love her. So I go on, every day, trying to make her see.

"I can't understand you," he said. "What makes you act this way? Where did it come from? You're nothing like your mother,"—though, just perhaps, even if the thought twisted his heart, she was—"and you're nothing like me."

"I am," she said in a low voice, looking down again. "I'm exactly like you."

When she spoke nonsense like that, it annoyed him more than anything else could have. And where anger could be kept in check, annoyance could not.

"Listen to me," he said.

"Don't lecture me again."

"Susanne! You will keep quiet and listen. Do you realize what you're doing, flirting with a man like Messerschmidt? Do you realize—has anything I've told you ever made an impression on you?—do you realize that except for an accident in time, that man could be one of the butchers who killed your mother?"

"Father, I've heard you say these things before. We've all heard you say them."

Now he'd begun, it was no longer any use not to go on. "Do you realize they oppressed and murdered and shipped to labor camps all the people I loved, all the people who were worthwhile in the world, until we rose up and wiped them out?" His hands folded down whitely on the arms of his chair.

"Where are your grandparents buried? Do you know? Do I?

Where is my brother? Where are my sisters?"

"I don't know. I never knew them."

"Listen—I was born in a world too terrible for you to believe. I was born to cower. I was born to die in a filthy cell under a police station. Do you know what a police station is, eh? Have I described one often enough? Your mother was born to work from dawn to night, hauling stones to repair the roads the army tanks had ruined. And if she made a mistake—if she raised her head, if she talked about the wrong things, if she thought the wrong thoughts—then she was born to go to a labor camp and strip tree bark for the army's medicines while she stood up to her waist in freezing water.

"I was born in a world where half a billion human beings lived for a generation in worship—in worship—of a man. I was born in a world where that one twisted man could tell a lie and send gigantic armies charging into death, screaming that lie. I was born to huddle, to be a cipher in a crowd, to be spied on, to be regulated, to be hammered to meet the standard so the standard lie would fit me. I was born to be nothing."

Slowly, Kimmensen's fingers uncurled. "But now I have freedom. Stepan Dubrovic managed to find freedom for all of us. I remember how the word spread—how it whispered all over the world, almost in one night, it seemed. Take a wire—twist it, so. Take some transistors—the army has radios, there are stores the civil servants use, there are old radios, hidden—make the weapon...and you are free. And we rose up, each man like an angel with a sword of fire.

"But if we thought Paradise would come overnight, we were wrong. The armies did not dissolve of themselves. The Systems did not break down.

"You take a child from the age of five; you teach it to love the State, to revere the Leader; you inform it that it is the wave of the future, much cleverer than the decadent past but not quite intelligent enough to rule itself. You teach it that there must be specialists in government—Experts in Economy, Directors of Internal Resources, Ministers of Labor Utilization. What can you do with a child like that, by the time it is sixteen? By the time it is marching down the road with a pack on its back, with the Leader's song on its lips? With the song written so its phrases correspond to the ideal breathing cycle for the average superman marching into the Future at one hundred centimeters to the pace?"

"Stop it, Father."

"You burn him down. How else can you change him? You burn him down where he marches, you burn his Leaders, you burn the System, you root out—everything!"

Kimmensen sighed. "And then you begin to be free." He looked urgently at Susanne. "Now do you understand what Messerschmidt is? If you can't trust my advice, can you at least understand that much? Has what I've always told you finally made some impression?"

Susanne pushed her chair back. "No. I understood it the first time and I saw how important it was. I still understood it the tenth time. But now I've heard it a thousand times. I don't care what the world was like—I don't care what you went through. I never saw it. You. You sit in your office and write the same letters day after day, and you play with your weapon, and you preach your social theory as though it was a religion and you were its high priest—special, dedicated, above us all, above the flesh. You tell me how to live my life. You try to arrange it to fit your ideas. You even try to cram Jem Bendix down my throat.

"But I won't have you treating me that way. When Anse talks to me, it's about him and me, not about people I never met. I have things I want. I want Anse. I'm telling you and you can tell Bendix. And if you don't stop trying to order me around, I'll move out. That's all."

Clutching his chair, not quite able to believe what he'd heard, knowing that in a moment pain and anger would crush him down, Kimmensen listened to her quick footsteps going away into her room.

IV

He was waiting out on the patio, in the bright cold of the morning, when Jem Bendix brought the plane down and picked him up. Bendix was pale this morning, and puffy-eyed, as though he'd been a long time getting to sleep and still had not shaken himself completely awake.

"Good morning, Joe," he said heavily as Kimmensen climbed in beside him.

"Good morning, Jem." Kimmensen, too, had stayed awake a long time. This morning, he had washed and dressed and drunk his coffee with Susanne's bedroom door closed and silent, and then he had come out on the patio to wait for Jem, not listening for sounds in the house. "I'm—I'm very sorry for the way things turned out last night." He left it at that. There was no point in telling Jem about Susanne's hysterical outburst.

Jem shook his head as he lifted the plane into the air. "No, Joe. It wasn't your fault. You couldn't help that."

"She's my daughter. I'm responsible for her."

Jem shrugged. "She's headstrong. Messerschmidt paid her some attention, and he became a symbol of rebellion to her. She sees him as someone who isn't bound by your way of life. He's a glamorous figure. But she'll get over it. I spent a long time last night thinking about it. You were right, Joe. At the moment, he's something new and exciting. But he'll wear off. The society'll see through him, and so will Susanne. All we have to do is wait."

Kimmensen brooded over the valleys far below, pale under the early morning mist. "I'm not sure, Jem," he answered slowly. He had spent hours last night in his chair, hunched over, not so much thinking as steeping his mind in all the things that had happened so suddenly. Finally, he had gotten up and gone into his bedroom, where he lay on his bed until a plan of action slowly formed in his mind and he could, at last, go to sleep.

"It's not the matter of Messerschmidt and Susanne," he explained quickly. "I hope you understand that I'm speaking now as someone responsible to all the families in this area, rather than as the head of any particular one. What concerns me now is that Messerschmidt is bound to have some sort of following among the immature. He's come at a bad time. He's in a good position to exploit this business in the Northwest."

And I'm going to die. Kimmensen had to pause before he went on.

"Yes, in time his bubble will burst. But it's a question of how long that might take. Meanwhile, he is a focus of unrest. If nothing happens to check him now, some people might decide he was right."

Bendix chewed his lower lip. "I see what you mean, Joe. It'll get worse before it gets better. He'll attract more followers. And the ones he has now will believe in him more than ever."

"Yes," Kimmensen said slowly, "that could easily happen."

They flew in silence for a few moments, the plane jouncing in the bumpy air, and then as Bendix slowed the vanes and they began to settle down into the valley where the office building was, Jem asked "Do you have anything in mind?"

Kimmensen nodded. "Yes. It's got to be shown that he doesn't have the population behind him. His followers will be shocked to discover how few of them there are. And the people wavering toward him will realize how little he represents. I'm going to call for an immediate election."

"Do you think that's the answer? Will he run against you?"

"If he refuses to run in an election, that's proof enough he knows he couldn't possibly win. If he runs, he'll lose. It's the best possible move. And, Jem...there's another reason." Kimmensen had thought it all out. And it seemed to him that he could resolve all his convergent problems with this one move. He would stop Messerschmidt, he would pass his work on to Jem, and—perhaps this was a trifle more on his mind than he'd been willing to admit—once Messerschmidt had been deflated, Susanne would be bound to see her tragic error, and the three of them could settle down, and he could finish his life quietly.

"Jem, I'm getting old."

Bendix's face turned paler. He licked his lips. "Joe—"

"No, Jem, we've got to face it. Don't try to be polite about it. No matter how much you protest, the fact is I'm almost worn out, and I know it. I'm going to resign."

Bendix's hands jerked on the control wheel.

Kimmensen pretended not to see it. For all his maturity, Jem was still a young man. It was only natural that the thought of stepping up so soon would be a great thrill to him. "I'll nominate you as my successor, and I'll campaign for you. By winning the election, you'll have stopped Messerschmidt, and then everything can go on the way we've always planned." Yes, he thought as the plane bumped down on the weathered plaza. That'll solve everything.

As Kimmensen stepped into his office, he saw Salmaggi sitting beside the desk, waiting for him. The man's broad back was toward him, and Kimmensen could not quite restrain the flicker of distaste that always came at the thought of talking to him. Of all mornings, this was a particularly bad one on which to listen to the man pour out his hysterias.

"Good morning, Tullio," he said as he crossed to his desk.

Salmaggi turned quickly in his chair. "Good morning, Josef." He jumped to his feet and pumped Kimmensen's hand. "How are you?" His bright eyes darted quickly over Kimmensen's face.

"Well, thank you. And you?"

Salmaggi dropped back into his chair. "Worried, Josef. I've been trying to see you about something very important."

"Yes, I know. I'm sorry I've been so busy."

"Yes. So I thought if you weren't too busy this morning, you might be able to spare ten minutes."

Kimmensen glanced at him sharply. But Salmaggi's moon of a face was completely clear of sarcasm or any other insinuation. There were only the worried wrinkles over the bridge of his nose and at the corners of his eyes. Kimmensen could not help thinking that Salmaggi looked like a baby confronted by the insuperable problem of deciding whether or not it wanted to go to the bathroom. "I've got a number of important things to attend to this morning, Tullio."

"Ten minutes, Josef."

Kimmensen sighed. "All right." He settled himself patiently in his chair.

"I was up in the northwest part of the area again on this last trip."

"Um-hmm." Kimmensen, sacrificing the ten minutes, busied himself with

25

thinking about Jem's reaction to his decision. Bendix had seemed totally overwhelmed, not saying another word as they walked from the plane into the office building.

"There's been another family burned out."

"So I understand, Tullio." Kimmensen smiled faintly to himself, understanding how Jem must feel today. It had been something of the same with himself when, just before the end of the fighting years, the realization had slowly come to him that it would be he who would have to take the responsibility of stabilizing this area.

"That makes seven in all, Josef. Seven in the past eight months."

"It takes time, Tullio. The country toward the northwest is quite rugged. No regime was ever able to send its police up there with any great success. They're individualistic people. It's only natural they'd have an unusual number of feuds." Kimmensen glanced at his clock.

It was a great responsibility, he was thinking to himself. I remember how confused everything was. How surprised we were to discover, after the old regime was smashed, that many of us had been fighting for utterly different things.

That had been the most important thing he'd had to learn; that almost everyone was willing to fight and die to end the old regime, but that once the revolution was won, there were a score of new regimes that had waited, buried in the hearts of suppressed men, to flower out and fill the vacuum. That was when men who had been his friends were suddenly his enemies, and when men whose lives he had saved now tried to burn him down. In many ways, that had been the very worst period of the fighting years.

"Josef, have you gone up there recently?"

Kimmensen shook his head. "I've been very occupied here." His responsibility was to all the families in the area, not to just those in one small section. He could never do his work while dashing from one corner of the area to another.

"Josef, you're not listening!" Kimmensen looked up and was shocked to see that there were actually glints of frustrated moisture in the corners of

Salmaggi's eyes.

"Of course I'm listening, Tullio," he said gently.

Salmaggi shook his head angrily, like a man trying to reach his objective in the midst of a thick fog. "Josef, if you don't do something, Messerschmidt's going to take an army up into the Northwesters' area. And I'm not sure he isn't right. I don't like him—but I'm not sure he isn't right."

Kimmensen smiled. "Tullio, if that's what's on your mind, you can rest easy. I am going to do something. This afternoon, I'm going to make a general broadcast. I'm going to call an election. I'm resigning, and Jem Bendix will run against Messerschmidt. That will be the end of him."

Salmaggi looked at him. "Of who?"

"Of Messerschmidt, of course," Kimmensen answered in annoyance. "Now if you'll excuse me, Tullio, I have to draft my statement."

That night, when he came home, he found Susanne waiting for him in the living room. She looked at him peculiarly as he closed the panel behind him.

"Hello, Father."

"Hello, Susanne." He had been hoping that the passage of a day would dull her emotional state, and at least let the two of them speak to each other like civilized people. But, looking at her, he saw how tense her face was and how red the nervous blotches were in the pale skin at the base of her neck.

What happened between us? he thought sadly. Where did it start? I raised you alone from the time you were six months old. I stayed up with you at night when your teeth came. I changed your diapers and put powder on your little bottom, and when you were sick I woke up every hour all night for weeks to give you your medicine. I held you and gave you your bottles, and you were warm and soft, and when I tickled you under the chin you laughed up at me. Why can't you smile with me now? Why do you do what you do to me?

"I heard your broadcast, of course," she said tightly.

"I thought you would."

"Just remember something, Father."

"What, Susanne?"

THE BURNING WORLD

"'There are a lot of us old enough to vote, this time.'"

V

Kimmensen shifted in his chair, blinking in the sunshine of the plaza. Messerschmidt sat a few feet away, looking up over the heads of the live audience at the mountains. The crowd was waiting patiently and quietly. It was the quiet that unsettled him a little bit. He hadn't said anything to Jem, but he'd half expected some kind of demonstration against Messerschmidt.

Still, this was only a fraction of the League membership. There were cameras flying at each corner of the platform, and the bulk of the electorate were watching from their homes. There was no telling what their reaction was, but Kimmensen, on thinking it over, decided that the older, more settled proportion of the League—the people in the comfort of their homes, enjoying the products of their own free labor—would be as outraged at this man as he was.

He turned his head back over his shoulder and looked at Jem.

"We'll be starting in a moment. How do you feel?"

Jem's smile was a dry-lipped grimace. "A little nervous. How about you, Joe?"

Kimmensen smiled back at him. "This is an old story to me, Jem. Besides, I'm not running." He clasped his hands in his lap and faced front again, forcing his fingers to keep still.

The surprisingly heavy crowd here in the plaza was all young people.

In a moment, the light flashed on above the microphone, and Kimmensen stood up and crossed the platform. There was a good amount of applause from the crowd, and Kimmensen smiled down at them. Then he lifted his eyes to the camera that had flown into position in front of and above him. "Fellow citizens," he began, "as you know, I'm not running in this election." There was silence from the crowd. He'd half expected some sort of demonstration of disappointment—at least a perfunctory one.

There was none. Well, he'd about conceded this crowd of youngsters to Messerschmidt. It was the people at home who mattered.

"I'm here to introduce the candidate I think should be our next League President—Secretary Jem Bendix."

This time the crowd reacted. As Jem got up and bowed, and the other cameras focussed on him, there was a stir in the plaza, and one young voice broke in: "Why introduce him? Everybody knows him."

"Sure," somebody else replied. "He's a nice guy."

Messerschmidt sat quietly in his chair, his eyes still on the mountains. He made a spare figure in his dark clothes, with his pale face under the shock of black hair.

Kimmensen started to go on as Jem sat down. But then, timed precisely for the second when he was firmly back in his chair, the voice that had shouted the first time added: "But who wants him for President?"

A chorus of laughter exploded out of the crowd. Kimmensen felt his stomach turn icy. That had been pre-arranged. Messerschmidt had the crowd packed. He'd have to make the greatest possible effort to offset this. He began speaking again, ignoring the outburst.

"We're here today to decide whom we want for our next president. But in a greater sense, we are here to decide whether we shall keep our freedom or whether we shall fall back into a tyranny as odious as any, as evil as any that crushed us to the ground for so long."

As he spoke, the crowd quieted. He made an impressive appearance on a platform, he knew. This was an old story to him, and now he made use of all the experience gathered through the years.

"We are here to decide our future. This is not just an ordinary election. We are here to decide whether we are going to remain as we are, or whether we are going to sink back into the bloody past."

As always, he felt the warmth of expressing himself—of reaffirming the principles by which he lived. "We are here to choose between a life of peace and harmony, a life in which no man is oppressed in any way by any other, a life of fellowship, a life of peaceful trade, a life of shared talents and ideals—or a life of rigid organization, of slavery to a high-sounding phrase and a remorseless system of government that fits its subjects to itself rather than pattern itself to meet their greatest good."

He spoke to them of freedom—of what life had been like before they were born, of how bitter the struggle had been, and of how Freemen ought to live.

They followed every word attentively, and when he finished he sat down to applause. He sat back in his chair. Jem, behind him, whispered:

"Joe, that was wonderful! I've never heard it better said. Joe, I...I've got to admit that before I heard you today, I was scared—plain scared. I didn't think I was ready. It—it seemed like such a big job, all alone.... But now I know you're with me, forever..."

Messerschmidt got up. It seemed to Kimmensen as though the entire crowd inhaled simultaneously.

"Fellow citizens." Messerschmidt delivered the opening flatly, standing easily erect, and then stood waiting. The attention of the crowd fastened on him, and the cameras dipped closer.

"First," Messerschmidt said, "I'd like to pay my respects to President Kimmensen. I can truthfully say I've never heard him deliver that speech more fluently." A ripple of laughter ran around the crowd. "Then, I'd like to simply ask a few questions." Messerschmidt had gone on without waiting for the laughter to die out. It stopped as though cut by a knife. "I would have liked to hear Candidate Bendix make his own speech, but I'm afraid he did." Messerschmidt turned slightly toward Bendix's chair. In Kimmensen's judgment, he was not using the best tone of voice for a rabble-rouser.

"Yes, Jem Bendix is a nice guy. No one has a bad word for him. Why should they? What's he ever done on any impulse of his own—what's he ever said except 'me, too'?"

Kimmensen's jaws clamped together in incredulous rage. He'd expected Messerschmidt to hit low. But this was worse than low. This was a deliberate, muddy-handed perversion of the campaign speech's purpose.

"I wonder," Messerschmidt went on, "whether Jem Kimmensen—excuse me; Jem Bendix—would be here on this platform today if Josef Kimmensen hadn't realized it was time to put a shield between himself and the citizens he calls his fellows. Let's look at the record."

Kimmensen's hands crushed his thighs, and he stared grimly at Messerschmidt's back.

"Let's look at the record. You and I are citizens of the Freemen's League. Which is a voluntary organization. Now—who founded the League? Josef Kimmensen. Who's been the only League President we've ever had? Who is the League, by the grace of considerable spellbinding powers and an electorate which—by the very act of belonging to the League—is kept so split up that it's rare when a man gets a chance to talk things out with his neighbor?

"I know—we've all got communicators and we've all got planes. But you don't get down to earth over a communicator, and you don't realize the other fellow's got the same gripes you do while you're both flapping around up in the air. When you don't meet your neighbor face to face, and talk with him, and see that he's got your problems, you never realize that maybe things aren't the way Josef Kimmensen says they are. You never get together and decide that all of Josef Kimmensen's fine words don't amount to anything.

"But the League's a voluntary organization. We're all in it, and, God help me, I'm running for President of it. Why do we stick with it? Why did we all join up?

"Well, most of us are in it because our fathers were in it. And it was a good thing, then. It still can be. Lord knows, in those days they needed something to hold things steady, and I guess the habit of belonging grew into us. But why don't we pull out of this voluntary organization now, if we're unhappy about it for some reason? I'll tell you why—because if we do, our kids don't go to school and when they're sick they can't get into the hospital. And do you think Joe Kimmensen didn't think of that?"

The crowd broke into the most sullen roar Kimmensen had heard in twenty-eight years. He blanched, and then raged crashed through him. Messerschmidt was deliberately whipping them up. These youngsters out here didn't have children to worry about. But Messerschmidt was using the contagion of their hysteria to infect the watchers at home.

He saw that suddenly and plainly, and he cursed himself for ever having put this opportunity in Messerschmidt's hands, But who would have believed that Freemen would be fools enough—stupid enough—to listen to this man?

Of course, perhaps those at home weren't listening.

"And what about the Northwesters' raids? Josef Kimmensen says there aren't any raids. He says we're settling our unimportant little feuds." This time, Messerschmidt waited for the baying laughter to fade. "Well, maybe he believes it. Maybe. But suppose you were a man who held this area in the palm of your hand? Suppose you had the people split up into little families, where they couldn't organize to get at you. And now, suppose somebody said, 'We need an army.' What would you do about that? What would you think about having an organized body of fighting men ready to step on you if you got too big for people to stand? Would you say, if you were that man—would you say, 'O.K., we'll have an army or would you say, 'It's all a hoax. There aren't any raids. Stay home. Stay split up?' Would you say that, while we were getting killed?"

The savage roar exploded from the crowd, and in the middle of it Messerschmidt walked quietly back to his chair and sat down.

Jem's fist was hammering down on the back of Kimmensen's chair.

"We should never have let him get on this platform! A man like that can't be treated like a civilized human being! He has to be destroyed, like an animal!"

Heartsick and enraged, Kimmensen stared across the platform at the blade-nosed man.

"Not like an animal," he whispered to himself. "Not like an animal. Like a disease."

Still shaken, still sick, Kimmensen sat in his office and stared down at his hands. Twenty-eight years of selfless dedication had brought him to this day.

He looked up at the knock on his open door, and felt himself turn rigid.

"May I come in?" Messerschmidt asked quietly, unmoving, waiting for Kimmensen's permission.

Kimmensen tightened his hands. "What do you want?"

"I'd like to apologize for my performance this afternoon." The voice was still quiet, and still steady. The mouth, with its deep line etched at one corner, was grave and a little bit sad.

"Come in," Kimmensen said, wondering what new tactic Messerschmidt would use.

"Thank you." He crossed the office. "May I sit down?"

Kimmensen nodded toward the chair, and Messerschmidt took it. "Mr. President, the way I slanted my speech this afternoon was unjust in many respects. I did it that way knowingly, and I know it must have upset you a great deal." His mouth hooked into its quirk, but his eyes remained grave.

"Then why did you do it?" Kimmensen snapped. He watched Messerschmidt's face carefully, waiting for the trap he knew the man must be spinning.

"I did it because I want to be President. I only hope I did it well enough to win. I didn't have time to lay the groundwork for a careful campaign. I would have used the same facts against you in any case, but I would have preferred not to cloak them in hysterical terms. But there wasn't time. There isn't time—I've got to destroy this society you've created as soon as I can.

After tonight's election, I will."

"You egomaniac!" Kimmensen whispered incredulously, "You're so convinced of your superiority that you'll even come here—to me—and boast about your twisted plans. You've got the gall to come here and tell me what you're going to do—given the chance."

"I came here to apologize, Mr. Kimmensen. And then I answered your question."

Kimmensen heard his voice rising and didn't care. "We'll see who wins the election! We'll see whether a man can ride roughshod over other men because he believes he has a mission to perform!"

"Mr. President," Messerschmidt said in his steady voice, "I have no idea of whether I am supplied with a mission to lead. I doubt it. I don't particularly feel it. But when I speak my opinions, people agree with me. It isn't a question of my wanting to or not wanting to. People follow me."

"No Freeman in his right mind will follow you!"

"But they will. What it comes down to is that I speak for more of them than you. There's no Utopia with room for men like you and me, and yet we're here. We're constantly being born. So there's a choice—kill us, burn us down, or smash your Utopia. And you can't kill more than one generation of us."

Messerschmidt's eyes were brooding. His mouth twisted deeper into sadness. "I don't like doing this to you, Mr. President, because I understand you. I think you're wrong, but I understand you. So I came here to apologize.

"I'm a leader. People follow me. If they follow me, I have to lead them. It's a closed circle. What else can I do? Kill myself and leave them leaderless? Someday, when I'm in your position and another man's in mine, events may very well move in that direction. But until the man who'll displace me is born and matures, I have to be what I am, just as you do. I have to do something about the Northwesters. I have to get these people back together again so they're a whole, instead of an aggregate of isolated pockets. I have to give them places to live together. Not all of us, Mr. President, were born to live in eagle rooks on mountaintops. So I've got to hurt you, because that's what the people need."

Kimmensen shook in reaction to the man's consummate arrogance. He remembered Bausch, when they finally burst into his office, and the way the great fat hulk of the man had protested: "Why are you doing this? I was working for your good—for the good of this nation—why are you doing this?"

Kimmenson had had too much. "That's enough of you and your kind's hypocrisy, Messerschmidt!" he choked out. "I've got nothing further I want to hear from you. You're everything I despise and everything I fought to destroy. I've killed men like you. After the election tonight, you'll see just how few followers you have. I trust you'll understand it as a clear warning to get out of this area before we kill one more."

Messerschmidt stood up quietly. "I doubt if you'll find the election coming out in quite that way," he said, his voice still as calm as it had been throughout. "It might have been different if you hadn't so long persisted in fighting for the last generation's revolution."

Kimmensen sat stiffly in Jem Bendix's office.

"Where's he now?" Bendix demanded, seething.

"I don't know. He'll have left the building."

Bendix looked at Kimmensen worriedly. "Joe—can he win the election?"

Kimmensen looked at Jem for a long time. All his rage was trickling away like sand pouring through the bottom of a rotted sack. "I think so." There was only a sick, chilling fear left in him.

Bendix slapped his desk with his hand. "But he can't! He just can't! He's bulldozed the electorate, he hasn't promised oBendix slapped his desk with his hand. "But he can't! He just can't! He's bulldozed the electorate, he hasn't promised one single thing except an army, he doesn't have a constructive platform at all—no, by God, he can't take that away from me, too!—Joe, what're we going to do?" He turned his pale and frightened face toward Kimmensen. "Joe—tonight, when the returns come in—let's be here in this building. Let's be right there in the room with the tabulating recorder. We've got to make sure it's an honest count."

VI

There was only one bare overhead bulb in the tabulator room. Bendix had brought in two plain chairs from the offices upstairs, and now Kimmensen sat side by side with him, looking at the gray bulk of the machine. The room was far down under the building. The walls and floor were cement, and white rime bloomed dankly in the impressions left by form panels that had been set there long ago.

The tabulating recorder was keyed into every League communicator, and every key was cross-indexed into the census files. It would accept one vote from each mature member of every League family. It flashed running totals on the general broadcast wavelength.

"It seems odd," Bendix said in a husky voice. "An election without Salmaggi running."

Kimmensen nodded. The flat walls distorted voices until they sounded like the whispers of grave-robbers in a tomb.

"Did you ask him why he wasn't?" he asked because silence was worse.

"He said he didn't know whose ticket to run on."

Kimmensen absorbed it as one more fact and let it go.

"The first votes ought to be coming in." Bendix was looking at his watch. "It's time."

Kimmensen nodded.

"It's ironic," Bendix said. "We have a society that trusts itself enough to leave this machine unguarded, and now the machine's recording an election that's a meaningless farce. Give the electorate one more day and it'd have time to think about Messerschmidt's hate-mongering. As it is, half the people'll be voting for him with their emotions instead of their intelligence."

"It'll be a close election," Kimmensen said. He was past pretending.

"It won't be an election!" Bendix burst out, slamming his hand on his knee. "One vote for Bendix. Two votes for Mob Stupidity." He looked down at the floor. "It couldn't be worse if Messerschmidt were down here himself, tampering with the tabulator circuits." Kimmensen asked in a dry voice: "Is it that easy?"

"Throwing the machine off? Yes, once you have access to it. Each candidate has an assigned storage circuit where his votes accumulate. A counter electrode switches back and forth from circuit to circuit as the votes come in. With a piece of insulation to keep it from making contact, and a jumper wire to throw the charge over into the opposing memory cells, a vote for one candidate can be registered for the other. A screwdriver'll give you access to the assembly involved. I studied up on it—to make sure Messerschmidt didn't try it."

"I see," Kimmensen said.

They sat in silence for a time. Then the machine began to click. "Votes, coming in," Bendix said. He reached in his blouse pocket. "I brought a communications receiver to listen on."

They sat without speaking again for almost a half hour, listening. Then Kimmensen looked at Bendix. "Those'll be his immediate followers, voting early," he said. "It'll even out, probably, when most of the families finish supper." His voice sounded unreal to himself.

Bendix paced back and forth, perspiration shining wetly on his face in the light from the overhead bulb. "It's not fair," he said huskily. "It's not a true election. It doesn't represent anything." He looked at Kimmensen desperately. "It's not fair, Joe!"

Kimmensen sighed. "All right, Jem. I assume you brought the necessary equipment—the screwdriver, the insulation, and so forth?"

After another half hour, Bendix looked across the room at Kimmensen. The removed panel lay on the floor at his feet, its screws rocking back and forth inside its curvature. "Joe, it's still not enough."

Kimmensen nodded, listening to the totals on the receiver.

"How many are you switching now?" he asked.

"One out of every three Messerschmidt votes is registering for me."

"Make it one out of two," Kimmensen said harshly.

They barely caught up with Messerschmidt's total. It was a close election. Closer than any Kimmensen had ever been in before. Bendix replaced the panel. They put out the room light and climbed back up to the ground level offices, bringing the chairs with them.

"Well, Joe, it's done." Bendix whispered though there was no one listening.

"Yes, it is."

"A thing like this creeps over you," Jem said in a wondering voice. "You begin by telling yourself you're only rectifying a mistake people would never make if they had time to think. You set a figure—one out of five. One person out of five, you say to yourself, would switch his own vote, given the chance. Then you wonder if it might not be one out of four —and then three.... Joe, I swear when I first suggested we go down there tonight, I hadn't a thought of doing—what we did. Even when I put the insulation and wire in my pocket, I never thought I'd—"

"Didn't you?" Kimmensen said. He felt disinterested. They'd had to do it, and they'd done it. Now the thing was to forget about it. "Good night, Bendix."

He left him and walked slowly through the corridors left over from another time. He went down the front steps and out into the plaza.

He found Messerschmidt waiting for him. He was standing in the shadow of the plane's cabin, and the plaza lights barely showed his face. Kimmensen stopped still.

Messerschmidt's features were a pale ghost of himself in the darkness. "Didn't you think I'd make spot-checks?" he asked with pity in his voice. "I had people voting at timed intervals, with witnesses, while I checked the running total."

"I don't know what you're talking about."

Messerschmidt nodded slowly. "Mr. Kimmensen, if I'd thought for a minute you'd do something like that, I'd have had some of my men in that building with you." His hands moved in the only unsure gesture Kimmensen had ever seen him make. "I had a good idea of how the vote would go. When it started right, and suddenly began petering out, I had to start checking. Mr. Kimmensen, did you really think you could get away with it?"

"Get away with what? Are you going to claim fraud—repudiate the election? Is that it?"

"Wait—wait, now—Mr. Kimmensen, didn't you rig the vote?"

"Are you insane?"

Messerschmidt's voice changed. "I'm sorry, Mr. Kimmensen. Once more, I have to apologize. I ought to have known better. Bendix must have done it by himself. I should have known—"

"No. No," Kimmensen sighed, "forget it, Messerschmidt. We did it together."

Messerschmidt waited a long moment. "I see." His voice was dead. "Well. You asked me if I was going to repudiate the election."

"Are you?"

"I don't know, yet. I'll have to think. I'll have to do something, won't I?"

Kimmensen nodded in the darkness. "Somehow, you've won and I've lost." Suddenly, it was all welling up inside him. "Somehow, you've arranged to win no matter what decent men do!"

"All right, Mr. Kimmensen. Have it your way."

"Whatever you plan to do now, I'll be home. If you should need me for a firing squad or some similar purpose."

Messerschmidt made an annoyed sound. "Mr. Kimmensen, you're notorious for your dramatics, but I think that's going too far." He walked away into the darkness.

Kimmensen climbed into his plane, sick at the night that covered him, and furious at Messerschmidt's ruthlessly sharp mind.

There was no one at home. He walked methodically through the house, doggedly opening Susanne's empty closets. Then he sat down in the living room with the lights off, staring out into the starlit, moonless night. He nodded sharply to himself.

"Of course," he said in the dark. "She'd be one of his timed voters." Then he sat for a long time, eyes straight ahead and focussed on nothing, every fold of his clothing rigidly in place, as though he were his own statue.

VII

Until, hours later, orange flowers burst in the valley below. He came erect, not understanding them for a moment, and then he ran out to the patio, leaning over the parapet. On the faint wind, he heard the distant sound of earth and houses bursting into vapor. In the valleys, fire swirled in flashes through the dark, and against the glare of burning trees he saw bobbing silhouettes of planes. Men were far too small to be seen at this distance, but as firing stabbed down from the planes other weapons answered from the ground.

Suddenly, he heard the flogging of a plane in the air directly overhead. He jumped back, reaching for his weapon, before he recognized Jem Bendix's sportster. It careened down to his landing stage, landing with a violent jar, and Bendix thrust his head out of the cabin.

"Joe!"

"What's happening?"

"Messerschmidt—he's taking over, in spite of the election! I was home when I saw it start up. He and his followers're cutting down everybody who won't stand for it. Come on!"

"What are you going to do?"

Bendix's face was red with rage. "I'm going to go down there and kill him! I should have done it long ago. Are you coming with me?"

Why not? Kimmensen grimaced. Why wait to die here?

He clambered into the plane and buckled his seat belt. Bendix flung them up into the air. His hands on the wheel were white and shaking as he pointed the plane along the mountain slope and sent them screaming downward. "They're concentrated around the office building, from the looks of it," he shouted over the whine of air. "I should have known he'd do this! Well, I'm League President, by God, and I'm going to settle for him right now!"

If you don't kill us first, Kimmensen thought, trying to check over his weapon. Bendix was bent over the wheel, crouched forward as though he wanted to crash directly into the plaza where Kimmensen could see running men.

They pulled out of the dive almost too late. The plane smashed down through the undergrowth behind the office building. Bendix flung his door open and jumped out while the plane rocked violently.

Kimmensen climbed out more carefully. Even here, in the building's shadow, the fires around the plaza were bright enough to let him see. He pushed through the tangled shrubbery, hearing Bendix breaking forward ahead of him. Ben cleared the corner of the building. "I see him, Joe!"

Kimmensen turned the corner, holding his weapon ready.

He could see Messerschmidt standing in a knot of men behind the wreckage of a crashed plane. They were looking toward the opposite slope, where gouts of fire were winking up and down the mountainside. Kimmensen could faintly hear a snatch of what Messerschmidt was shouting: "Damn it, Toni, we'll pull back when I—" but he lost the rest. Then he saw Bendix lurch out of the bushes ten feet behind them.

"You! Messerschmidt! Turn around!"

Messerschmidt whirled away from the rest of the men, instinctively, like a great cat, before he saw who it was. Then he lowered the weapon in his hand, his mouth jerking in disgust. "Oh—it's you. Put that thing down, or point it somewhere else. Maybe you can do some good around here."

"Never mind that! I've had enough of you."

Messerschmidt moved toward him in quick strides. "Listen, I haven't got time to play games." He cuffed the weapon out of Bendix's hand, rammed him back with an impatient push against his chest, and turned back to his men. "Hey, Toni, can you tell if those Northwesters're moving down here yet?"

Kimmensen's cheeks sucked in. He stepped out into the plaza, noticing Bendix out of the corners of his eyes, standing frozen where Messerschmidt had pushed him.

Kimmensen came up to Messerschmidt and the man turned again. His eyes widened. "Well, Mr. Kimmensen?"

"What's going on?"

Messerschmidt grunted. He pointed up the mountain. "There they are. I suppose they knew they had to move fast once I repudiated the election. They began airdropping men about a half hour ago. They're thick as flies up there, and they'll be coming down here as soon as they're through mopping up. That ought to be in a few minutes."

"Northwesters."

"That's right, Mr. Kimmensen."

"Well."

Messerschmidt smiled thinly. "I suppose you've guessed Susie's at my house?"

"Will she be all right?"

Messerschmidt nodded. "It's fortified. That's our next holding point when we fall back from here." His face was grave.

"Isn't there any chance of stopping them?"

Messerschmidt shook his head. "None. They're military specialists, Mr. Kimmensen. We don't have any trained men."

"I see."

Messerschmidt looked at him without any perceptible triumph in his eyes.

THE BURNING WORLD

"It seems, Mr. Kimmensen, that they have men like us in the Northwest, too. Unfortunately, theirs seem to have moved faster."

"What're you going to do?"

Messerschmidt looked up the mountain and shrugged. "Nothing. We got some of them in the air, but the rest are down. We may have weapons as good as theirs, but they know how to use them in units. It's quite simple. We'll try to hold and kill as many as we can when they come at us. We'll keep retreating and holding as long as we can, and when we reach the sea, if we get that far, we'll drown."

Kimmensen frowned. "Their men are concentrated on that mountain?"

"Yes."

"And you're just going to stand still and let the League be wiped out?"

"Just what, Mr. Kimmensen, would you like me to do?" Messerschmidt looked at him in fury. "I don't have time to train an army of our own. They've got us cold."

"Messerschmidt, I see eight men here with weapons."

"As far as anything we can accomplish goes, we might as well use them to toast sandwiches."

"We can scour that mountainside. Down to bare rock."

Messerschmidt blanched. "You're joking."

"I am not!"

"There are people of ours up there."

"There are people of ours all through this area. When the Northwesters are finished up there, they'll fan out and burn them all down, a little bit at a time."

Messerschmidt looked at Kimmensen incredulously. "I can't do it. There's a chance some of our people up there'll be able to slip out."

"By that time, the Northwesters'll be down here and dispersed."

Messerschmidt started to answer, and stopped.

"Messerschmidt, if you're going to do anything, you'd best do it immediately."

Messerschmidt was shaking his head. "I can't do it. It's murder."

"Something much more important than human life is being murdered on that mountain at this moment."

"All right, Kimmensen," Messerschmidt exploded, "if you're so hot for it, you give the order! There're something like a hundred League families up there. Half of them're still alive, I'd say. If the election's void, you're still president. You take the responsibility, if you can."

"I can."

"Just like that."

"Messerschmidt, the defense of freedom is instantaneous and automatic."

"All right, Mr. Kimmensen," Messerschmidt sighed. He turned to his men. "You heard him. It's his order. Aim at the mountain." He bared his teeth in a distorted laugh. "In freedom's name—fire!"

Kimmensen watched it happen. He kept his face motionless, and he thought that, in a way, it was just as well he hadn't long to live.

But it was done, and, in a way, his old dream was still alive. In a way, Messerschmidt's hands were tied now, for in the end the Freemen defeated the trained armies and no one could forget the lesson in this generation.

He looked down at the ground. And in a way, Messerschmidt had won, because Kimmensen was dying and Messerschmidt had years.

That seemed to be the way of it. And Messerschmidt would someday die, and other revolutions would come, as surely as the Earth turned on its axis and drifted around the sun. But no Messerschmidt—and no Kimmensen—ever quite shook free of the past, and no revolution could help but borrow from the one before.

Well, Bausch, Kimmensen thought to himself as the face of the mountain slowly cooled and lost color, I wonder what we'll have to say to each other?